The *Let's-Read-and-Find-Out Science* book series was originated by Dr. Franklyn M. Branley, Astronomer Emeritus and former Chairman of the American Museum–Hayden Planetarium, and was formerly co-edited by him and Dr. Roma Gans, Professor Emeritus of Childhood Education, Teachers College, Columbia University. Text and illustrations for each of the books in the series are checked for accuracy by an expert in the relevant field. For more information about Let's-Read-and-Find-Out Science books, write to HarperCollins Children's Books, 10 East 53rd Street, New York, NY 10022, or visit our website at www.letsreadandfindout.com.

Let's Read-and-Find-Out Science® is a trademark of HarperCollins Publishers.
Collins is an imprint of HarperCollins Publishers.

Sid the Science Kid: Everybody, Move Your Feet!

Library of Congress catalog card number: 2009942013
ISBN 978-0-06-185264-0
Typography by Rick Farley
10 11 12 13 14 SCP 10 9 8 7 6 5 4 3 2 1

❖
First Edition

STAGE 1

Jim Henson's
the Science KID

Everybody, Move Your Feet!

Adapted by Jodi Huelin

Collins
An Imprint of HarperCollinsPublishers

Good morning, Sid!
Sid has exciting news to share.
"I'm going to make a pillow fort, and do nothing but watch my favorite TV show—*Fire Dog Brigade*—all weekend long. I'll sit in front of the TV all day and night!"

"Isn't it a brilliant idea? Hmm, well, Mom and Dad probably won't love this 'just watch TV' plan. But why?"

"I've got to know—what's the big deal with TV? Why can't I *watch it all weekend*?"

"Breakfast time! TV! TV! TV! TV!" Sid yells, running into the kitchen.

"Good morning, Sid!" Mom says.

Sid greets his family. "Hey, Zeke and Mom. Hi, Dad!"

Sid tells his family his super, brilliant plan for the weekend.

"I have the *best* idea in the world. I'm going to bring a TV into my room, sit on my bed, and watch *Fire Dog Brigade* all weekend long!"

Sid is all smiles and excitement as he awaits their response.

"*All* weekend long? Sid, you *cannot* watch TV all weekend long," Mom answers.

"All that TV wouldn't be good for you," Dad says. "Your body would get really tired."

EXCUSE ME?!

Maybe Mom and Dad didn't hear Sid. How could he get tired? Sid wouldn't be *moving*, he'd be *watching*!

"Because your body needs to move," Dad answers. "You need to exercise your muscles, like . . ."

NO WAY!

"This!" Dad says, striking a pose and doing deep-knee bends. Sid's mom agrees.

"If you didn't move at all and just watched TV, your body would turn to mush," she says.

Sid doesn't quite understand.
"I know–I'll investigate at school!
Maybe my friends can help me figure this out!"

Sid jumps out of the car, excited to see his friends.
Gabriela, Gerald, and May are waiting for him on the playground.
Sid asks the question of the day:
"Do you know anyone who exercises?"

I'M ROVING REPORTER SID, WITH TODAY'S SURVEY!

"I do. My dad and my dog Chester exercise together!" answers Gerald. "They run around this big field—but my dog is a lot faster than my dad."

May knows someone who likes to exercise, too.

"My aunt Karen does tai chi," May says, doing a cool tai chi move.

Sid asks Gabriela next.

"My brother plays soccer . . . and I play with him!" she says.

Now Sid knows what some people do for exercise.

Maybe Teacher Susie can help Sid and his friends learn more.

"Come on in, we've got a lot to learn today!" Teacher Susie sings.

The kids take their seats.

"Who has something they want to talk about?" Teacher Susie asks.
"On the playground, we talked about exercise," Gabriela responds.
Sid explains how he wants to watch *Fire Dog Brigade* all weekend.
"Except my mom and dad say it's not good for my body."

"To stay healthy and strong you have to exercise your whole body," Teacher Susie says.

"Even your feet?" asks Gabriela.

"And your arms?" asks Gerald.

"Yes! Exercise is even good for your brain. It helps you think better," Teacher Susie explains.

It's time for an investigative exercise with a special *outside* Super Fab Lab on the playground!
"Grab your journals and let's go!" Teacher Susie says.

INVESTIGATE, EXPLORE, DISCOVER!

Teacher Susie describes the right and wrong ways to exercise.
"There are many ways to exercise your body," she says.
"The important thing is to just move your body and have *fun*."
WOW!

"You'll know you're moving around enough when you can feel your heart beating fast," Teacher Susie continues.

Sid and his friends put their hands over their hearts. They can't feel anything! That's because right now their hearts are beating s-l-o-w-l-y. But after some exercise, they will try again!

Sid leads the group in some stretching and warming up.

Then everyone shows a favorite way to move. One, two, three—GO!

Teacher Susie does jumping jacks.

Gabriela kicks
a soccer ball.

Sid does a robot dance
with a robot voice. "I like
pretending to be a robot
making pancakes!"

May pretends to garden
with her grandpa, planting
and weeding and watering.

Gerald tap dances and sings.
(Hey–that's exercising his lungs, too!)

It's your turn–what's your favorite way to move your body?

"You're all exercising and building strong muscles," Teacher Susie says encouragingly. "Everyone put your hands over your hearts and observe if it's beating the same or faster than before."

May says her heart is beating really fast.

And Gerald and Gabriela agree that they are breathing really fast.

"You're a scientist—you can try this, too!" says Sid.

Sid and his friends grab their journals. It's time to draw some observations!

Gerald draws a picture of himself dancing.

"I'm drawing myself working in my grandpa's garden," May offers. "Picking up every single weed is hard work, but it's fun!"

Gabriela draws a picture of herself playing soccer.

Sid draws himself as a robot, his heart beating fast and really hard. "Boom, boom, boom, boom!" Sid says.

Sid can't believe the school day is over already—there's Grandma to pick him up.

"Hey, Grandma! We learned about exercise today!"

Sid had no idea playing, dancing, and using his body was so important for staying healthy. Staying healthy is fun!

Sid can't wait to tell his family all about his *new* brilliant idea.

"Scientist in the house! We learned how exercise is good for our bodies in school today," Sid says. "It gives us energy and helps our heart and arms and even our brain!"

But what is Sid's great idea, his parents and grandma wonder?

"Instead of watching *Fire Dog Brigade*, our whole family can act out *Fire Dog Brigade*! Hooray!"

Do you remember when Sid and his friends did an experiment in class, and they felt their hearts beating? *(Boom! Boom! Boom!)* Well, that's called a *pulse*.

Hey! What's a pulse?

A pulse is the beating of your heart.

Wait! I want to know more! What else can you tell me about my pulse?

A pulse is the number of times that your heart beats each minute.

What else is a pulse called?

Your pulse is also called your "heart rate."

What is happening inside my body to make a pulse?

Your pulse can change minute to minute, depending on what you're doing! Like Sid showed you, your pulse speeds up when you're exercising. And that's a good thing! Exercising your body also means that you're exercising your heart. Did you know that your heart is a muscle? Well, it is! It's a very, very important muscle. It pumps blood all around your body so it can work the way it should. Your heart is INSIDE your body, but you can feel it OUTSIDE. Feeling your pulse is a fun way to observe your heart at work!

Whoa, I can observe my pulse?

Yes! By measuring your pulse, you can find out how fast your heart is beating. Here's what you do (you'll need some help from an adult):

There are a few spots where you can find your pulse. Place two fingers on your wrists or on the side of your neck. You have found your pulse when you can feel a slight beating underneath your skin.

Using a watch or a clock with a second hand, count how many beats you feel in 15 seconds. Remember, those beats are the beats from your heart. This is where your mom or dad or another adult can be handy. Have someone count with you! Then, ask the adult to multiply that number by four. **That's your pulse!**

It's time for today's Sid Survey!

Hey there, scientists! There are just *sooo* many ways to exercise I can barely count them! But what about you?

For a super special Sid Survey, draw a picture of yourself doing *your* favorite exercises! Ask your friends and your family about *their* favorite ways to exercise, too. Then add those pictures to your journal. Do you want to find out even more ways to exercise? Ask your teacher and your doctor, too, at your next checkup. And add drawings of those exercises to your journal. Then the next time you think of saying, "Hey, Mom, I'm *bored*!" take a look in your journal for the oh-so-many fun ways to get up and move your body! Then give yourself a pat on the back—you did a good job!

Hooray for exercise!